KATE MCMULLAN

Papa's Song

PICTURES BY

JIM MCMULLAN

FARRAR STRAUS GIROUX • NEW YORK

For Mary Pope Osborne,
who said bears

Text copyright © 2000 by Kate McMullan
Pictures copyright © 2000 by Jim McMullan
All rights reserved
Distributed in Canada by Douglas & McIntyre Ltd.
Color separations by Hong Kong Scanner Arts
Printed and bound in the United States of America by Berryville Graphics
Typography by Filomena Tuosto
First edition, 2000

3 5 7 9 11 10 8 6 4 2

Library of Congress Cataloging-in-Publication Data
McMullan, Kate.
  Papa's Song / Kate McMullan ; pictures by Jim McMullan. — 1st ed.
    p.   cm.
  Summary: After Grandma, Grandpa, and Mama Bear unsuccessfully try to sing Baby Bear
to sleep, Papa Bear finds just the right song.
  ISBN 0-374-35732-3
  [1. Bears—Fiction. 2. Babies—Fiction. 3. Sleep—Fiction. 4. Father and child—Fiction.]
I. McMullan, Jim, 1936– ill. II. Title.
PZ7.M47879Pap   2000
[E]—dc21   99-34556

Baby Bear can't go to sleep.

"I will sing you to sleep, Baby Bear,"
says Granny Bear.
She picks Baby Bear up
and plops down in the rocker
and sings Baby Bear a song.

I'm your granny, I know best.
Time for little bears to rest.
Day is over, evening's here,
Go to sleep, my dumpling dear.

Granny Bear sighs a sleepy sigh.

But Baby Bear doesn't.

Along comes Grandpa Bear.
"I will sing you to sleep, Baby Bear,"
says Grandpa Bear.
He takes Baby Bear from Granny Bear
and walks to the window
and sings Baby Bear a song.

I'm your grandpa, wise and gray.
You have had a busy day.
Now the moon shines down its light,
And it's time to say good night.

Grandpa Bear says, "Good night."

But Baby Bear doesn't.

Along comes Mama Bear.
"I will sing you to sleep, Baby Bear,"
says Mama Bear.
She takes Baby Bear from Grandpa Bear
and walks to the mouth of the bear cave
and sings Baby Bear a song.

I'm your mama, up since dawn.
How I wish that you would yawn.
Stars are blinking in the skies,
Telling you to close your eyes.

Mama Bear closes her own sleepy eyes.

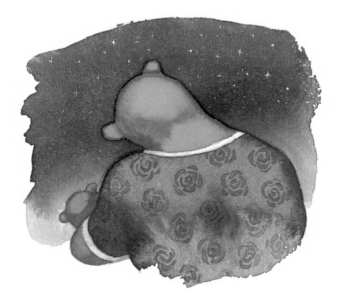

But Baby Bear doesn't.

"My turn," says Papa Bear.
He takes Baby Bear from Mama Bear
and carries Baby Bear out to the bear boat.

Papa Bear poles Baby Bear down the river.
Riffles slap the side of the bear boat,
slup, slup, slup.

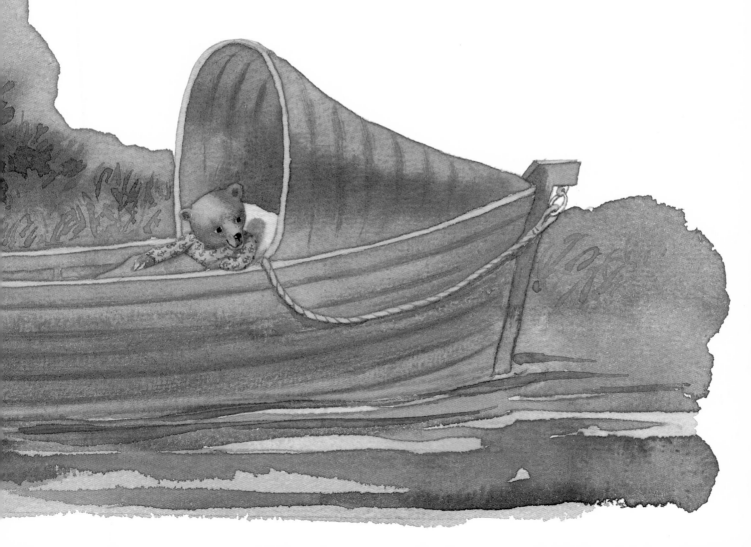

Three little fish wriggle by and disappear
beneath the water, *bloop, bloop, blip.*
A frog croaks, *CHUG-A-RUM! CHUG-A-RUM!*
A faraway frog answers, *chug-a-rum!*
chug-a-rum!

A pair of otter pups going home to their den slide into the river, *sssplish! sssplash!* A duck paddles by, talking softly to itself, *wack wack, wack wack.* A night owl calls, *hoooo! hoooo! hoooo!*

And the crickets chirp on and on and on.

"However did you do it?" asks Granny Bear
when Papa Bear brings Baby Bear home.
Papa Bear smiles. "I knew the right song."

Then all the Bears kiss Baby Bear
and tuck Baby Bear into a soft,
warm bear bed.
"Dream sweet dreams, Baby Bear,"
says Papa Bear.

And Baby Bear does.